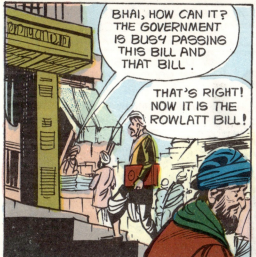

* CLOSING OF SHOPS AS A MARK OF SORROW OR PROTEST

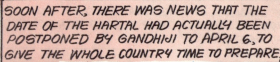

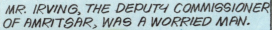

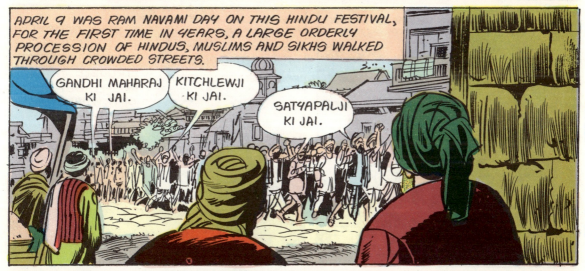

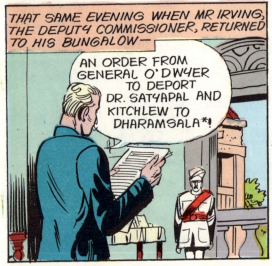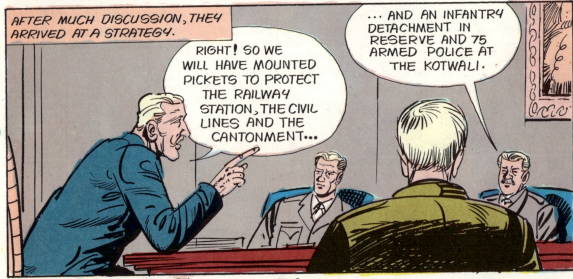

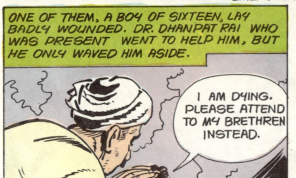

DISORGANISED, LEADERLESS, THE CROWD HAD NOW BECOME A MOB. GROUPS OF TEN TO THIRTY MEN ARMED WITH LATHIS AND SPIKES ATTACKED THE RAILWAY GOODS YARD...

...AND THE TELEGRAPH OFFICE.

AS THE CROWDS IN HALL BAZAAR PASSED THE NATIONAL BANK OF INDIA, SOMEONE THREW A STONE AT ONE OF ITS WINDOWS.

THAT SEEMED TO ACT LIKE A SIGNAL. THE MOOD OF THE CROWD CHANGED. SUDDENLY IT TURNED VIOLENT.

THE MANAGER AND HIS ASSISTANT, TWO ENGLISHMEN, WERE BEATEN TO DEATH AND THE BANK WAS SET ON FIRE.

TWO OTHER BANKS IN THE NEIGHBOURHOOD WERE ALSO ATTACKED AND LOOTED. INTERESTINGLY ENOUGH, THESE BANKS WERE VERY CLOSE TO THE KOTWALI WHICH WAS IN THE CHARGE OF TWO INDIAN OFFICERS. THEY DID NOT LIFT A FINGER TO HELP.

TO BUY ANY AMAR CHITRA KATHA OR TINKLE COMIC NOW SIMPLY

Call Toll Free on **1800-233-9125**
(Mon-Fri 9.30 am to 6.00 pm IST
or Leave a voice mail)

SMS '**ACK BUY**' to '**575758**'
and we will call you back

Log on to www.amarchitrakatha.com
to select your favourite comics and
read the story of the week online

**More Thrills
More Excitement
More Mystery
More Humour**

The World of Amar Chitra Katha Heroes just got more exciting!

Introducing
The NEW Animated DVDs

- Hanuman to the Rescue
- Birbal The Wise
- Tales of Shivaji
- The Pandavas in Hiding

To order — Log on to www.amarchitrakatha.com or Call Toll free on 1800-233-9125 or SMS '**ACK BUY**' to '**575758**'

SUBSCRIBE NOW!

SUBSCRIBER DETAILS

Name _____
Date of Birth _____
Address _____
_____
City _____ Pin _____
State/Country _____
Phone _____
Email _____
Signature _____
☐ I have subscribed earlier to ACK/Tinkle. (Please tick)

SUBSCRIPTION PLAN

TINKLE Magazine
☐ 1 Year
☐ 2 Years
☐ 3 Years

TINKLE Digest
☐ 1 Year
☐ 2 Years
☐ 3 Years

COMBO Subscription
☐ 1 Year
☐ 2 Years
☐ 3 Years

PAYMENT OPTIONS

☐ Pay by Money Order
☐ Pay by Cheque/DD
  a) Enclosed cheque/DD in favour of 'Amar Chitra Katha Pvt. Ltd.'
  b) Please add Rs. 15 for Non-Mumbai cheques
☐ Pay by credit card
  a) Card type: ☐ Visa ☐ Master
  b) Please charge Rs. _____ to my credit card number _____
  c) Expiry date _____
  d) Card member's signature _____
☐ Pay by VPP (Value Payable Post) – Pay cash on delivery of 1st issue to the postman (Additional charges of Rs. 24)

Mail to: Amar Chitra Katha Pvt. Ltd. 14, Marthanda, 84, Dr. Annie Besant Road, Worli, Mumbai – 400 018.
Tel.: 022-6629 6999/838 Fax: 022-6629 6900
Email: tinklesubscription@ack-media.com
SMS: ACK BUY to 575758

Subscribers receive their copies before the newsstands!!

TINKLE Magazine
72 pages of new stories every month!

	Stand Price	India	Overseas
1 Year	~~Rs. 240~~	Rs. 225	Rs. 1125
2 Years	~~Rs. 480~~	Rs. 440	Rs. 2025
3 Years	~~Rs. 720~~	Rs. 640	Rs. 2925

TINKLE Digest
96 pages of the best stories from the past issues of Tinkle magazine!

	Stand Price	India	Overseas
1 Year	~~Rs. 480~~	Rs. 450	Rs. 1575
2 Years	~~Rs. 960~~	Rs. 880	Rs. 2925
3 Years	~~Rs. 1440~~	Rs. 1280	Rs. 4050

COMBO Subscription
Best of both new and old Tinkle!*

	Stand Price	India	Overseas
1 Year	~~Rs. 720~~	Rs. 640	Rs. 2250
2 Years	~~Rs. 1440~~	Rs. 1260	Rs. 4275
3 Years	~~Rs. 2160~~	Rs. 1830	Rs. 6075

* Tinkle magazine and digest arrive separately.

You can also subscribe at www.tinkleonline.com. Tinkleonline users get upto 1750 bonus Tinkle Gold coins on subscribing online!

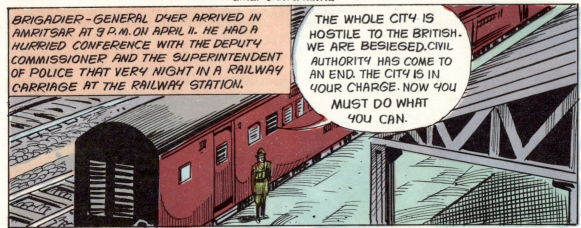

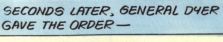

THERE WERE FOUR OR FIVE SMALL GAPS AMONG THE BUILDINGS SURROUNDING THE BAGH AND PEOPLE STARTED RUNNING TOWARDS THOSE.

ON DYER'S ORDER THE GUNS WERE DIRECTED STRAIGHT AT THE NARROW GAPS THROUGH WHICH PEOPLE WERE TRYING TO ESCAPE.

PEOPLE CONTINUED TO FALL, BUT STILL THE SHOOTING DID NOT STOP.

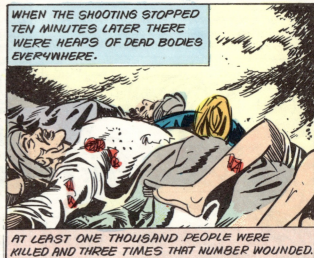
WHEN THE SHOOTING STOPPED TEN MINUTES LATER THERE WERE HEAPS OF DEAD BODIES EVERYWHERE.

AT LEAST ONE THOUSAND PEOPLE WERE KILLED AND THREE TIMES THAT NUMBER WOUNDED.

THE WOUNDED CRIED OUT.
WATER!
WATER!

BUT THE SOLDIERS JUST MARCHED AWAY.

EVEN IN A WAR, WOUNDED ENEMY SOLDIERS ARE GIVEN FIRST AID. BUT AT JALLIANWALLA BAGH UNARMED CITIZENS WERE ABANDONED TO DIE IN MISERY.